Puffin Books

Britt the Boss

Bossy? You've never seen anything like it! Bossy Britt Blainey is the bossiest kid in the whole of Mango Street Primary School. She tells everyone what to do – even her friend Rosie Tucker.

So, when the class has to think of ways to raise money for a charity, Britt the Boss decides she's got the best idea of all. That is, until Nanny the goat nibbles through the goal-post, Fiona the Frog lands on Mr Walsnott's head, and the cats start chasing the guinea-pigs . . .

Also by Margaret Clark

Pugwall
Pugwall's Summer
The Big Chocolate Bar
Tina Tuff
Famous for Five Minutes
Ripper and Fang
Plastic City
Hold My Hand – Or Else
Fat Chance
Living with Leanne
Calvin the Clutterbuster
Ghost on Toast
Tina Tuff in Trouble
The Biggest Boast
Hot or What – Another Fat Chance

Also in the Mango Street series

Weird Warren
Butterfingers
Wally the Whiz Kid

Britt the Boss

Margaret Clark

Illustrated by Bettina Guthridge

Puffin Books

Puffin Books
Penguin Books Australia Ltd
487 Maroondah Highway, PO Box 257
Ringwood, Victoria 3134, Australia
Penguin Books Ltd
Harmondsworth, Middlesex, England
Viking Penguin, A Division of Penguin Books USA Inc.
375 Hudson Street, New York, New York 10014, USA
Penguin Books Canada Limited
10 Alcorn Avenue, Toronto, Ontario, Canada M4V 3B2
Penguin Books (N.Z.) Ltd
182-190 Wairau Road, Auckland 10, New Zealand

First published by Penguin Books Australia, 1995
10 9 8 7 6 5 4 3 2 1
Copyright © Margaret Clark, 1995
Illustrations Copyright © Bettina Guthridge, 1995

Typeset in 13/15 Adobe Garamond by Midland Typesetters, Maryborough, Victoria
Made and printed in Australia by Australian Print Group, Maryborough, Victoria

National Library of Australia
Cataloguing-in-publication data:

Clark, M.D. (Margaret Dianne), 1943–
Britt the boss.

ISBN 0 14 036269 X.

I. Guthridge, Bettina. II. Title.

A823.3

For Jemima and Sara, with love

Contents

Chapter One

The Bossiest Mango

Bossy? You've never seen anything like it!

Britt is the bossiest kid in our class. In our school. Probably in the whole world. She tells everyone what to do and how to do it. Even Miss Perret, our teacher. Britt seems to know when Miss Perret doesn't feel like arguing, like when she's tired – with big dark circles under her eyes. Or when she's jittery and chewing her pencil. That sometimes happens when she's had a fight with her boyfriend, 'cause he usually calls in at lunch-time then. If you stand on the railings you can see them holding hands next to his motorbike. Her boyfriend's a biker, you see. Which is weird, because Miss Perret looks pretty boring, and he looks exciting.

Anyway, you have probably got a handle on Britt now. She wants her own way *all* the time, hits on you when you're feeling down, and generally is a bit of a pain. The good thing about her is that she does have 'fine leadership qualities' as Miss Perret *keeps* reminding us. At least Britt's better than Tabitha Walsnott, the Principal's daughter. He thinks that Tabitha should be boss of the school. Personally I think she's about as entertaining as an ant farm without the ants.

I'm not sure why kids do what Britt tells them. It's probably easier to give in than argue. That's why she can boss Miss Perret sometimes and other kids can't, and before you can say go and suck your socks you're doing what she wants.

And because no other kids want to sit with her, *I* have to, otherwise she won't be my friend. Who needs a bossy friend, you're thinking? The major problem is that our mums are best friends. We were even *born* at the same time, in the *same* hospital, and our mums shared a room together. But I guess I'm so used to Britt being bossy that I don't let it stress me. It'd be too complicated *not* to be her friend because the Blaineys (her family) live next door, three streets away from our school.

And speaking of our school . . . well, it's very old. It's in an inner Melbourne suburb. It's called Mango Street Primary, in case you don't know already. Maybe there was a Mango tree once, but now there isn't even a gumtree in sight.

The nearest school to us is called Chilten Primary; we call the kids from there the 'Chillers'. They call us the 'Mannas' or the 'Fruit Loops'. When we play netball against them it's a real war. Most times we win. That's when having Bossy Britt, who's also a fantastic goalie, is a real advantage. Even the Chillers are scared of her.

Our school has two storeys and our room is on the top floor. Britt and I sit in the first desk near the door so's she can see what's going on in the teachers'

OUR SCHOOL

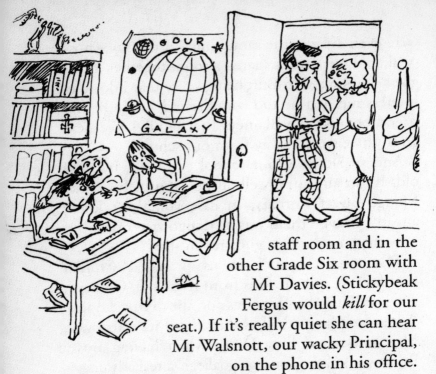

staff room and in the other Grade Six room with Mr Davies. (Stickybeak Fergus would *kill* for our seat.) If it's really quiet she can hear Mr Walsnott, our wacky Principal, on the phone in his office. Then she can tell Tabitha the school's business which really gets up her nose. Most schools have offices on the ground floor but Mr Walsnott likes the view across the park to the river. That's why the main office is downstairs and his is upstairs.

Sometimes I think I'd like another friend. I'd like to sit up the back of the room near Warren 'Worry Wart' Wilson, or in the middle near Justin 'Copy Cat' Day. But Britt is *very* possessive. She sees who goes in and out of my house because her lounge-room faces the street and her bedroom faces straight into mine. She sees where I

go. She's in the same netball team, the Junior
Black Panthers, in the same gym class, in the
same brownie pack. So I'm stuck with her
whether I like it or not! My name should be
Rosie Stucker, not Rosie Tucker.

And another thing – people say we look good
together because we're so opposite. Britt's got
straight, black hair, no freckles, sharp blue eyes
and is long and thin. Britt loves sport and nearly
always wears her sports gear. I'm short, with funny
hair (which I hate) and almost black eyes (which I
hate) although most people tell me that my eyes
are beautiful. (Yuk.) I would *love* to look like Britt.
But I'd hate to be that bossy! Which brings me to the
point of my story . . . All the kids call Britt 'Bossy
Boots' (behind her back, not to her face – they
wouldn't be game). Once Boldy wrote 'Britt is a
Bossy B . . .' on the school wall with chalk. He
didn't get to finish the last word because Mr
Walsnott came round the corner and roared . . .

Boldy dropped the chalk in fright but we all knew he meant to write 'Boots'.
I wouldn't be game enough to write on the school wall. I'm not a wimpette but I don't like to be yelled at by Mr Walsnott. I guess school Principals have to be bossy and yell their heads off or they wouldn't

pass their 'Boss of the School' exams and get their own offices.

'Rosie,' said Britt next to me in English class, 'stop dreaming and pass me your red pencil.' She needed it to underline the verbs in her sentence and she'd forgotten hers. It was just before morning recess, so by the time she'd borrowed my red pencil *all* day, it would be just a stump. I could argue, but she'd twist it round to make me look mean. 'What? Not give me even a tiny loan of your red pencil?' she'd say in a very loud voice. Miss Perret would look annoyed at being interrupted from correcting homework, and Tabitha would snigger and Fergus would stare. It wasn't worth it. I gave Britt my pencil. She never said 'please' or 'thank you' either. She just demanded. I was beginning to think that something would have to be done about Britt the Boss.

we found this hanging in MR Walsnott's garage!! You'd think he'd have it hanging in his office...

(Dig the middle name!!)

BOSS OF THE SCHOOL
Randolph Herbert Walsnott

ON THIS DAY, PASSED WITH 'FLYING COLOURS' AND DISTINCTIONS IN AUTHORITY

MR Lear A.J.A.
HEAD BOSS OF SCHOOLS

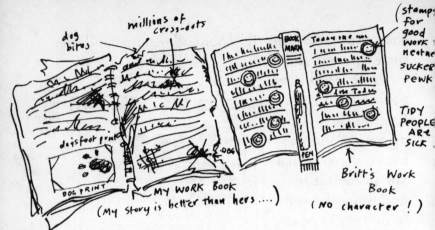

dog bites

millions of cross-outs

(stamps for good work neatness

SUCKER PEWK

dog's foot print

DOG PRINT

MY WORK BOOK

(My story is better than hers....)

BOOK MARK

PEN

Britt's Work Book

(NO character!)

TIDY PEOPLE ARE SICK

Britt ruled neat lines under her English verbs. My lines looked like wriggling worms and my writing looked like a spider had rap-danced across the page. Sitting next to Britt made me feel nervous because she was so good at everything. My dad is always saying, 'Give her the flick, Rosie.' Or 'Britt's bad news.' Or 'she sucks your personality like a giant vacuum cleaner.' I can't tell him I'm too scared of her to tell her to get lost. Plus mum keeps saying, 'Don't be silly. They're best friends.' Or 'Britt's good for Rosie: she brings her out of her shell.'

Dad just looks at me and shrugs. 'Some friend-ships should die a natural death,' he says.

I looked at Britt's work as she underlined the wrong word.

'Now look what you've made me do, Rosie. You bumped me. Give me your rubber.'

I handed it over. If Britt kept bossing me for

the rest of the year I'd have nothing left! It was only the third of May. I'd turn into a full-on wimp by the end of the year!

Then it was morning recess.

'Hey, Rosie, want to play French Skippy?' yelled Stacey. She needed someone to stand at one end with the elastic round their knees. She had

Der! Give me a look!

the other end. She was so clumsy when she jumped that she always preferred to take an end.

'She's not playing with *you*, she's playing with *me*,' snapped Britt. 'And we're playing Downball, not dumb French Skippy.'

'I wouldn't mind playing French Skippy,' I said. 'I'd like to be an elastic holder. My hand's too sore to play Downball today.'

'Der! Give me a look.'

Britt grabbed my hand, jerking it hard, and I gave a yelp.

'Leave her alone,' said Big Mac, giving Britt a shove.

'Mind your own business, Fatso,' said Britt.

I decided to stick up for myself.

'I'm tired of you bossing me around. *I* want to choose the game.'

'Okay, then. What do you want to play? And *not* Skippy.'

'Er . . .' I said. 'What about "Puss in the Corner"?'

'Sure. With two people.'

'We could get some more.'

'By the time you find some, recess'll be over. Think again, Rosie.'

When she was sarcastic like that I just clammed up. My brain couldn't think at all.

'What about "Chain Tiggy"?'

'No. Too dumb.'

'What about . . . er . . .'

But it was too late. The bell had gone. Britt glared at me.

'What a waste of time,' she said, tossing her black hair. 'We could've played two games of Downball, Rosie. Sometimes you drive me up the wall.'

And sometimes you drive me round the twist, nuts, off the planet and round the bend, I thought, but I didn't say it out loud, or Britt'd pinch me.

After recess our new student-teacher came into class. We'd been expecting him earlier but he'd phoned to say that his car had broken down. Most student-teachers are young and pretty. This one was old and ugly. At least thirty. He was very pale and serious, with weird-looking hands.

'This is Mr Cole,' said Miss Perret.

'Mr Cole? Does your dad own all the supermarkets?' snickered Tabitha.

Miss Perret glared at Tabitha. Then she wrote, *Our new teacher is Mr Cole* on the board.

'He looks like a dweeb,' said Bossy Britt to me. 'What a wimp.'

Sometimes she can be so *rude*.

'I think he looks nice,' I whispered back. 'Sort of like a Russian ballet dancer, or a romantic poet.'

'Der!' she muttered. 'Trust you to think he's nice. I prefer a *hunk*.'

Good morning Grade six Mango...

We said good morning to Mr Cole in our usual way: 'Goo . . . ood mor . . . ning . . . Mis . . . ter . . . Cole.'

'Good morning, Grade Six Mango,' he said in a chilly voice. His eyes regarded us carefully. 'I will be with you for three weeks.'

His voice was creepy. He wasn't like the other student-teachers we'd had at all! He had a beaky nose and thin, tight lips. It was obvious to me

that teaching wasn't his first career choice. He'd probably wanted to be a robot engineer or a brain surgeon. Or maybe he'd wanted to work in his family's supermarket chain. I had to agree with Britt. Major dweeb. His clothes were really dorky: a patterned jumper and grey check trousers. No one had taught him to put clothes together, or if they had, he wasn't listening.

He sat up the back and stared at Miss Perret as she gave us a Maths lesson. I could feel his eyes boring into the back of my head but I wasn't game to turn round and see.

'Oooh, he gives me the creeps,' said Kylie at lunch-time when we were picking sides for netball.

'I think he's escaped from a mental asylum,' whispered Justin, who's always a bit ghoulish. 'He's probably got a knife in his briefcase and a bomb in his pocket.'

'I've seen his face on telly,' said Boldy. 'He's a serial killer.'

'Nuts,' said Bossy Britt, who'd appointed herself team captain again. 'He's just the student-teacher. He doesn't scare *me*.'

'Well, he scares *me*,' said Stacey. 'He looks like the creep out of *Psycho*. Don't you think so, Rosie?'

'I think . . .' I began.

'She doesn't think *anything*,' said Bossy Britt impatiently. 'Are we going to stand here all day or play netball? And are you boys gonna perv on us all the time? Clear off. Rosie, you're defence. Stacey, you can watch.'

You might be wondering how everyone lets Britt boss them on the netball court. Problem is, she's the best. She knows I'm good at defence. She knows Stacey will keep dropping the ball so she can only play for two or three minutes. When Britt is the captain, no matter how bad her team is, she usually makes you play better because she's so excellent herself.

check out the fangs !!
(could easily pass
as a python . . . .)

After lunch we had our first lesson with Mr Cole. Usually student-teachers never take a lesson on the first day. They sit up the back and learn everyone's names. But Miss Perret said he was 'keen to get his teeth into some teaching', and he could take us for Science. She really meant 'get his *fangs* into us', because his two front teeth were sharp and pointed like real snake's fangs.

'You.' He was pointing at me. 'You can give out the Science books.'

Bossy Britt put up her hand. 'You don't understand, Mr Cole. *I'm* the Science book monitor.'

'You don't understand, little-girl-in-the-front-with-the-black-hair, *I'm the teacher.*'

They glared at each other. Bossy Britt gritted her teeth and her face turned a dull red. She wasn't used to being told off by anyone. Justin gave a really stupid giggle and that made her even madder. I thought she was going to *explode*. Mr Cole was about to change Mango Street Primary for ever . . . Britt the Boss had finally met her match!

Chapter Two
Snakes Alive

'Get the Science books!' said Mr Cole firmly.

I went to the cupboard where Miss Perret kept the books in a neat pile. I was shaking so much that I thought I'd drop them all over the floor. There was dead silence as I gave them out.

Not one kid spoke as we learnt about reptiles. Boy, did Mr Cole know about snakes and lizards!

'Er . . . excuse me, Mr Cole,' interrupted Miss Perret from the back of the room, 'but the tiger snake is dark brown with black bands, not grey.' She

17

sounded really peeved. It wasn't often that the student-teacher would know more than she did. It was really getting up her nose.

'This is often the case,' said Mr Cole, 'but remember, snakes are similar to chameleons. They take on the colour of their habitat. So, if a two-metre tiger snake was living in a woodpile, like the one I disturbed on my uncle's farm, it could easily adapt. This one was silvery grey with darker bands.'

'A grey western adder,' snapped Miss Perret.

'*Not* in Southern Victoria, Miss Perret.'

Miss Perret tightened her lips. She would gallop straight to the library during the break. She hated to be wrong.

'Hey, Mr Cool,' said Horace. 'Did the snake go for you? Did it?'

We all cracked up. Mr Cool. Good one.

'The name is *Cole*. C.O.L.E. And yes, it reared up, ready to strike.'

'Wow. What did ya do, Sir?' asked Justin.

Miss Perret stomped noisily from the back down to the front and flounced out the door. She was going to do some speed reading on snakes or my name isn't Rosie Tucker. We had nearly finished drawing common snakes and lizards when she came back *very* quietly. That meant Mr Cole was a snake expert, after all.

'Yep,' said Worry Wart at afternoon recess, 'I

think he's really a snake in disguise, a mutant from a planet where . . .'

'Don't be stupid,' I said.

'I wouldn't sit in the front seat, Rosie,' he continued. 'He might lean over to correct your work and bite you. I'd move if I were you.'

'Go bite *yourself*, Worry Wart. Rosie's not shifting,' snapped Bossy Britt.

There was nowhere to shift anyway, except up with Worry Wart at the back. He sat in the far corner near the window so that if there was a fire, earthquake or some other disaster he could leap out. Only trouble is that we're on the top storey!

'During the three weeks that Mr Cole will be with us he would like you to work on a pet project of his,' said Miss Perret after recess when we were back in class.

'Breeding mice,' hissed Bossy Britt out of the corner of her mouth. 'He eats 'em for breakfast.'

'Oh, *yuk*!' I said. 'That's a very sick joke, Britt.'

'I'm not joking.'

I stared at Mr Cole. Eating mice? Nah . . . it was too gross.

'Rosie,' said Mr Cole, staring at me. 'Do your eyes usually pop out like that or have you suddenly developed a thyroid problem?'

I tried to answer but the more he stared at me the more my throat tightened up and I couldn't say anything.

'No matter,' he said. 'I . . .'

Bossy Britt put up her hand with a flourish. 'She thinks you eat mice for breakfast, Mr Cole.' The class tittered.

He answered Britt with a cold stare. 'I do. I do. Fried with a little butter, on toast.'

Bossy Britt went a pasty white.

'Enough about my eating habits. I am the Chairman on the Eventide Home for the Aged Fund-Raising Committee. I want this class, Six Mango, to think of ways to raise money for this charity, and we'll put them into action as a class project.'

'I hate these mature-aged students,' whispered Britt. 'He's too old to learn teaching. He should be in the Eventide Home as a resident.'

'You were saying something, Britt Blainey?' His voice was cutting.

'For a major project like this we need a committee,' said Bossy Britt. 'And of course I will be the president.'

She was *always* the president of every committee we'd ever had as long as I could remember. To give her credit, Miss Perret always asked if anyone else wanted to be the president but no one ever challenged Bossy Britt. Ever. It didn't seem fair. I looked across at the others. No one was arguing. She would be the president as usual. I wondered what it'd be like to be the president of something. Not the USA, that was mind-boggling. Something small, like a class project. It couldn't be that hard, could it?

'So. No one else wants to be the president of the committee?' said Mr Cole, his eyes roving round the room. 'That's a shame.'

His gaze came to rest on me. Go on, it said. I'd like to try but Britt'd give me a dead arm after school. But then anything was better than Mr Cole's stare. I put my hand up.

'Yes, Rosie? You want to be president?'

Britt kicked me hard under the desk. I stifled a yelp.

'I . . . er . . . it'd be a good idea to . . . have an election,' I said. 'Then we could all have a vote. It'd be good practice for . . . well . . . er . . .'

There was a startled murmur behind me. I shrank further into my seat. How embarrassing!

'Do you want nominations, or will everyone

write their choices on a piece of paper?'

'I don't mind,' I mumbled, trying to shift away from Britt's pinching fingers.

Miss Perret was looking pleased for the first time since Mr Cole had taken over the class. Perhaps they'd learn to like each other after all. Perhaps she'd drop her bikie boyfriend with the long hair and go with Mr Cole, and she'd change him from a cold-blooded snake into a warm-blooded human. Sort of like the princess and the frog.

'Everyone, write one name on a page from your pad of the person whom you'd like to be president of the committee,' said Mr Cole. 'Fold it over and hand it to me, please.'

Soon he'd put a pile of folded votes on the table.

'Two people have to count them,' said Bossy Britt furiously.

Mr Cole raised his eyebrows. 'Should it be Miss Perret and myself? No, I think not. What about Boldani and Wilson?'

Warren 'Worry Wart' Wilson looked like a hypnotised rabbit. His eyes bulged, his nose quivered, and his mouth made funny little mewing sounds. He hated responsibility. He was a full-on worrier from way back. Fergus the Stickybeak tried to cure him once – he's improved but it'd take time to cure him totally. Warren whimpered.

'Could someone else do it?'

'Can't you count, Wilson?'

'Yes, but . . .' he squeaked nervously, 'I . . .'

'Come on, boy, stop messing about and get on with it.'

They both stood at the table counting the votes. Mr Cole actually winked at Miss Perret! She looked a little flustered but then she gave a nod of approval. She was always trying to get Warren to do things so that he could build up his confidence. She was always trying to get Boldy to do something he couldn't mess up, too. Boldy is very nice but sometimes he can *act* a little . . . *thick*. I think he thinks if he acts thick she won't make him do anything, which is often true: she gives up on him.

'And?' asked Mr Cole.

Warren looked scared stiff.

The class waited with bated breath. You could've heard a feather fall. Warren finally announced the winner.

'The committee president is . . . Rosie.'

Bossy Britt gave me a cold stare. If looks could kill, I'd be dead!

RENOSAURUS

WARREN

Chapter Three

The Big Surprise

'Excuse me,' said Bossy Britt in a deadly calm voice. 'Mr Cole, I would prefer to work in my own group with my own *friends*.'

She gave me a sideways glare at the same time. 'It could be a competition to raise the most money.'

'What do you think, Rosie?' asked Mr Cole.

I was still stunned. Who'd voted for *me*? Did they think I had hidden leadership qualities? Or had they wanted to stop Britt being the boss of the class as usual?

'Rosie? Are you there? Earth to Rosie, come in, please.'

'All right,' I mumbled. 'I don't mind if we have a competition. It will probably raise more money

for the old people. Yes. I think it's a good idea.'
And at least Britt wouldn't keep pinching me for the
rest of Year Six if she had her own group.

'Are you trying to say, Britt, that we need two
presidents?' asked Mr Cole coldly.

'I suppose it's a good idea,' said Miss Perret,
looking thoughtfully at me. Did she mean that I'd
probably mess up being a president? Or did she
think that Britt'd leave me alone if she had her
own group? It's so hard to read a teacher's mind!

Mr Cole sighed.

'All right. Two groups. The group that raises
the most money for the Eventide Home will
attend the special dinner and present the cheque.
Only . . .' he paused, looking at Miss Perret, 'I

don't think we need two presidents, do we? We need two group leaders, Rosie and Britt, and Rosie can also be the overall president of the project. What do you think?'

Miss Perret thought quickly. After the snake episode she didn't want to look stupid. She nodded.

'What do you think, class?' she said. 'Hands up those who agree.' A zillion hands shot skywards. (They were so stunned they'd have agreed to *anything*.)

So that's how I came to be president of the Eventide Home for the Aged Fund-Raising Committee for Grade Six Mango. The first time I'd ever been chosen for anything important in my life. I looked at Britt. She had her head down and her arm covering what she was writing. It wasn't taking her long to get organised, I thought, when I saw her pass the note. It accidentally came back through me, and I saw what it said before she grabbed it. She had written, 'If you don't join *my* group I'll rearrange your face.' I didn't have a hope.

At the end of the day I had heaps of notes saying that seven kids wanted to be in my group. I had one from Worry Wart, one from Kylie and Stacey, one from Boldy, Sticks and Justin, and, big surprise, one from Big Mac. I'd thought Horace Morris might join, but he was too scared of Britt. Eight kids, including me, against the others. It was going to be hard. I had to think of a slogan, and fast. One for the whole project that would bind us together because we were really all working towards the same thing. I put up my hand.

'Yes, Rosie?'

'I've been thinking about the project, Miss Perret.'

After all, she was still in charge and we were now in the middle of silent reading. Mr Cole was up the back again, writing something in a notebook. Everyone stopped reading and stared at me. I'm not used to that. It made me feel uncomfortable, but if I was going to be president of the project I couldn't look like I was scared. I took a deep breath.

'I think we need a slogan for the overall project,' I said, 'and I think it should be, "*Go, Mango*".'

I think we need a slogan...

'Huh, that's dumb,' said Britt. But Miss Perret beamed and wrote it up on the board in huge orange letters. GO MANGO.

'We can make a banner,' said Cornflake, who's good at art.

'Yeah. And stickers. We could sell them to the rest of the school,' added Justin.

'Sure,' sneered Britt. 'Where're ya gonna get money to buy stickers?'

Personally I thought it was a good idea. We could work on it. I smiled at Justin to show him I thought that it was a great money-spinner.

Fergus put up his hand. 'Is it okay if I swap to Rosie's group?' he said. 'I'd like to make stickers.'

'Me too,' said Horace.

I was so happy that I thought I'd burst. Two more people. That made ten, nearly half the grade. Wow.

I sent round a note to say we'd have a meeting after school at my house. We weren't allowed to talk any more because we hadn't finished our silent reading period. That was when I got a note back from this other boy, Piggsy, who loved to eat even more than Big Mac. He wanted to join my group, too.

'Why?' I wrote back.

''Cause I've tasted your mum's choc-chip cookies and they're the *best*,' he wrote. I'd forgotten the cake stall last year at school.

Unreal. *Eleven* kids.

Mum was really pleased when I brought my group home after school. She's not like some mothers, worrying about dirt on the carpets or crumbs all over the floor and the furniture. She's

happiest when she's feeding hordes of people. Up to now I'd mainly only ever brought home Britt who didn't like sweet things. (My dad says she'd improve her sour temper if she tucked into a few choc-chip cookies.) But Britt's a bit of a health freak. She works out and is learning Tai Chi so she can boss us even more. (Well, that's what we think.) Mum let some kids use the phone to tell their parents where they were, and started piling cakes, biscuits and slices onto plates. Piggsy was looking disappointed when no choc-chip cookies appeared. I whispered in mum's ear and she found three for him, so he was happy. We sat in the family room while mum brought in more heaped plates of jelly slice, hedgehog, honey joys, and cans of cola. She was thrilled that I had all these new friends. And no Britt for a change made her surprised.

'How are we going to make piles of money?' said Worry Wart, getting straight to the point.

'You could make fudge and toffee,' said Mum. 'There's a really good market for homemade sweets.' Her eyes were gleaming. I could just see her stirring and whipping and blending toffees and

marshmallows and fudge. She looks like a crazy scientist when she cooks, with pots on the stove and trays of half-cooling sweets all over the place. She wears her special lucky apron which covers her from neck to ankle. In big red writing it says, *Born to Cook*. Her hair all goes into curly wisps from the steam and her nose goes bright red from the heat, but my mum's only really happy when she's 'creating' in her kitchen, as Dad says.

'Mum,' I reminded her, 'we're supposed to do this ourselves. It's our Go Mango school project.'

'Mr Cole didn't exactly say that,' said Piggsy. 'He didn't say that mothers couldn't cook.'

'And mothers are parents, and parents are part of our school,' added Big Mac.

'Yeah,' said Justin. 'Fathers are, too.'

'We could work together,' said Mum. 'We could have a big bake-up after school tomorrow night. I could supervise and you could do most of the work.'

'Yeah,' said Fergus. 'Then we could sell all the stuff at school on Friday and make heaps of money!'

'We need to advertise, then,' said Kylie, 'make posters to put up in school so that all the kids will bring their money.'

'And we'll have to pay back Rosie's mum for the ingredients,' added Stacey, 'or it's not fair.'

'Who said anything about "fair"?' said Big Mac. 'Britt'll fight dirty, I can tell you that.'

Mum looked surprised. Then she looked worried. 'I thought she was Rosie's best friend,' she said. 'They've been close for years and years. Our families have been best friends for ages.'

'Well, here's the truth,' said Big Mac. 'I think Rosie's better off without Britt for her best friend right now. She's gonna be *mean*.'

Mum looked shocked.

'Hey,' said Boldy, 'let's work out how much sugar and stuff we'll use and how much profit there'll be when we've sold everything.' (His dad and mum own the local fruit shop. He knows about profit and loss.) So we spent the rest of the time working on posters and our lists of ingredients.

The next day at school we put up our posters. GIANT TOFFEE AND SWEET SALE. MONEY IN AID OF OLD PEEPLE. WE NEED YOUR HELP SO BUY, BUY, BUY, TOMORROW, 10 am, SHELTER SHED.

'Huh,' said Britt when she saw the notice. 'Poxy idea. Is that all you're going to do?'

'What are *you* doing then, smartypants?' asked Fergus boldly.

'None of your business, stickybeak.'

Fergus *did* tend to stick his nose in where it wasn't wanted.

'That's not how you spell "people",' said this nerd from Six Silver who thinks he knows every-thing.

'*So?*'

Fergus grabbed him by the arm. Britt grabbed Fergus by the hair. Horace trod on Britt's foot. It would turn into a really full-on brawl if something didn't . . .

'Hey. What's going on? HAVEN'T YOU KIDS HEARD THE BELL AND WHY AREN'T YOU MOVING TOWARDS THOSE DOORS DO YOU NEED ROCKETS UNDER YOU NOW STOP THAT MESSING AROUND AND GET GOING OR YOU'LL SPEND THE REST OF YOUR SCHOOL LIVES PICKING UP PAPERS DO YOU HEAR ME?'

Phew. I never thought I'd be glad to see Mr Walsnott!

That night after school we made a million toffees, a million pieces of fudge and a million marshmallows. Well, it seemed like it. Big Mac and Piggsy were useless: they kept licking all the spoons and bowls. They said they were Official Tasters. Worry Wart kept fretting about the hygiene in Mum's kitchen. He was sure we had to have some sort of government permit to cook for the general public and that we'd all be sued and have to go to jail.

'Warren,' said Mum for the billionth time, 'we are *not* cooking for the general public, we are cooking for Mango Street Primary, and my kitchen is *clean*.'

My mum is very patient but Warren was starting to drive her up the wall. Fergus was also getting Mum a little edgy. He kept peering in her cupboards and poking his nose into the pantry. Finally we were finished.

'I can mind some of the sweets overnight,' offered Piggsy eagerly.

'No way,' said Boldy. 'They'd all be eaten. My dad can bring his van around tomorrow early and take them all to school.'

It was settled. Being a group leader was easy. I hadn't made one decision yet. But niggling in the back of my mind was a major worry. What had Britt and her group been doing next door?

Chapter Four

Britt Gets Sneakier!

The next day we set up our stall in the shelter shed. We were allowed out at ten o'clock to start selling. The Preps came first, clutching their money. But what was this? Some of them were wearing bright orange stickers with GO MANGO written on in black. While we'd been setting up, Britt and her group had gone from grade to grade selling the stickers!

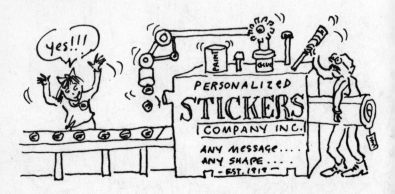

'But that was *my* idea!' wailed Justin. 'And how did she get professional stickers printed so quickly?'

'Her dad,' I sighed.

Britt overheard. 'Remember my uncle Brian has a printing business, Rosie? He makes sticky labels for a living!'

Anyway, it meant that all the kids in the school had less money to spend on sweets if they had bought a sticker for twenty cents. But by the time Grade Six arrived we'd nearly sold everything. Our tin was still really full with money, despite the sticker problem.

'Want to buy a sticker?' said Britt. 'I've got eight left.'

'No way,' yelled Justin. 'You pinched my idea.'

'That's a change, pinching an idea from *you.*'

Justin was boiling mad. He usually copies from everyone else. Britt had outsmarted him and he didn't like it.

'I'll buy a sticker,' I said. 'After all, it *is* for a common cause. Would you like to buy a toffee, Britt? Or a marshmallow?'

No one from her group was buying anything. They were standing back, smirking.

'Buy something from *you?*' sneered Britt. 'You must be nuts. Here's your sticker and give us twenty cents.'

I was so shocked at her nastiness that I handed it over. We still had a dozen toffees, twenty marshmallows, and ten packets of fudge. But the kids in Britt's group weren't buying. And all the other kids had spent their money.

'Just what I need,' said Mr Cole, who was wearing a GO MANGO sticker. 'A dozen toffees, twenty marshmallows, and ten packets of fudge. I'll take the lot.'

Being skinny he didn't have to worry about his figure like Miss Perret, who'd only bought one small toffee. She was skinny, too, but only because she ate an apple and an orange for lunch and drank black coffee. If she got fat she probably

wouldn't fit on the back of her boyfriend's bike and he'd dump her. That's what Stacey said.

Anyway, thanks to Mr Cole, we'd sold all our stock and our stall was a big success.

'Huh,' sneered Britt. 'You'll be lucky if you've made fifty dollars. *We've* made much more than that.'

'So how much have you made, then?' challenged Boldy. 'Go on. How much?'

She just smiled and wouldn't say. Who cares. Our stall had been a huge success. We still had to pay Mum ten dollars for the ingredients which left us thirty-six dollars and twenty-two cents. Proudly I handed the tin full of money to Mr Cole. He checked it and wrote the amount in a notebook.

Now we had to think of another way to make money.

'What about a long-jump contest?' said Sticks who has the longest legs in the whole school and is the best long-jumper.

'No one would pay to enter,' said Stacey.

'I know. What about a baby photo contest? Guess who the baby is? And we could charge an entry fee.'

That sounded a great idea. We made posters during Art. BABY PHOTO COMPETITIN. BRING YOUR BABY PHOTO. GUESS ALL THE BABBIES. WIN A PRIZE.

Britt looked over my shoulder.

'Competition is "i-o-n",' she smirked. 'And you don't spell "babies" like that.'

'You were never a baby so how would you know?' said Boldy. 'You were born under a cabbage, mean and nasty, looking just like you do now.'

She looked to see if Miss Perret was watching and gave Boldy a quick kick.

'Britt,' said the cold voice of Mr Cole, as Boldy struggled not to yell out, 'your group needs you. Go.'

I fixed up the spelling and we cut out some round, chubby babies from magazines to make our posters look cool. Bossy Britt had asked Miss Perret if they could work on their project in the multi-purpose room. I overheard Cornflake tell Sticks that they were going to swear Miss Perret to secrecy about their project. None of the kids in Britt's group would tell, either. She'd bash 'em up after school, even the boys. She couldn't bash up Miss Perret, of course. But if Miss Perret took a vow of silence she wouldn't tell, either.

They could keep their secret. So far we were winning with thirty-six dollars and twenty-two cents.

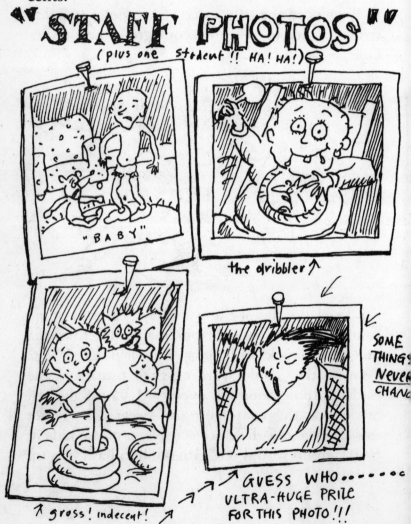

"STAFF PHOTOS"
(plus one student !! HA! HA!)

"BABY"

the dribbler ↑

↗ gross! indecent! ↗

SOME THINGS NEVER CHANGE

↗ ↗ GUESS WHO........ ULTRA-HUGE PRIZE FOR THIS PHOTO !!!

We put our posters up around the school. Kids started bringing baby photos with their names on the back. You should've seen Miss Perret when she was a baby. Skinny and hairless like a bald chook. Mr Cole was as round as a basketball with little googly eyes and chubby cheeks. He sure had changed, unless it was a fake photo. That's what Horace said. He reckoned Mr

↑ Yes - of course ↑ ME ♡♡

Cole was a mass murderer on the run and he'd brought a fake photo so we couldn't dob to the cops. But Mr Walsnott was the most disgusting baby of all. He was big and fat with dribble all down the front of his bib and one tooth right in the middle of his mouth like a fang. Boy, was he an *ugly* baby. Tabitha tried to nick the photo of her dad, but

Miss Perret saw her and made her put it back. I felt sorry for Tabitha. It'd be awful to have a fang-faced baby as your *father*.

They say babies don't really change much, and that you can tell who's who. Some you could. Britt looked mean and nasty, spitting out her dummy and glaring at the camera. (She'd let her group enter our contest 'cause she was sure she could guess all the babies and win.)

'You haven't changed much, Rosie,' said Mr Cole, pointing at my photo. I'd been born with lots of thick, curly, dark hair. My photo showed me at nine months trying to smile at the camera. I guess everyone would know it was me.

There were heaps of photos. We stuck them all on the wall in the multi-purpose room, which meant

that Britt's group had to work in the library. Kids could stare at the photos all recess and all lunch-time but they couldn't enter unless they paid fifty cents. Then they were given a form with all the numbers from one to fifty (*two* grade sixes: we'd had to limit the whole school from entering because it would've got too complicated).

I had wanted the entry fee to be twenty cents but Mr Cole said that fifty was fair, because we had to buy the prizes for first, second and third. They had to be decent prizes or the whole school'd get mad and rip off our heads to use for bowling balls.

Finally after hours of hard work we came up with the winners. It was bad news. Bossy Britt had won first prize, a kid from the other grade six class had come second and Worry Wart had come third, only Mr Cole explained that that wasn't legal because Worry Wart could've known the answers, and no one in our group was eligible to enter. We had to give Worry Wart back his fifty cents. That meant the third prize went to another kid in Six Silver which wasn't so bad except she was a real whiner called Winnie. It would be lovely if a nice kid'd won something, I thought. Sometimes I wonder if there is justice in the world.

We had to give Bossy Britt a brand new tape recorder because Mr Cole had bought it on 'special' from his brother's shop. The second and third prizes were vouchers for CDs. It all came to sixty dollars which left us with sixty-four dollars and forty cents.

'Peanuts,' said Bossy Britt, when it was announced. 'Totally peanuts.'

Just *what* was *she* planning?

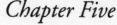

Chapter Five

Britt's Big Secret

'You still can't guess, can you?'

Britt looked superior.

'No. I can't guess,' I said.

'The whole school will know soon when we put up *our* posters at lunch-time. Then you'll be sorry, Rosie Rabbit.'

The suspense was terrible. Britt the Boss had everyone stressing right out. Her group was walking round looking smug, and when they were in class they spent the whole time passing notes to each other when the teachers weren't looking. Fergus tried to sneak a look but Britt saw him and gave him a really hard pinch on the arm. If there is ever a Miss Universe Pinching Contest, Britt will win hands down.

The bell rang and everyone jumped to their feet, 'cause they wanted to see what Britt was going to do. Where would she put the first poster? What would it say? Everyone thumped and yelled down the passage.
'HEY. WHAT'S ALL THIS ROW IN THE PASSAGE DON'T YOU KNOW I'M ON THE PHONE AND HOW MANY TIMES HAVE I TOLD YOU NOT TO RUN INSIDE DO YOU WANT ME TO MAKE YOU

CONCRETE SHOES SO YOU ALL HAVE TO HOBBLE FOR THE REST OF YOUR LIVES BE QUIET OR ELSE!' roared Mr Walsnott.

Britt walked very slowly with all her group right behind her. She went to the stairs and took each step at the pace of a snail until she finally reached the bottom, with everyone crowding behind. When she reached the noticeboard she unrolled the large poster she'd had under her arm, and carefully pinned it up. I stood on tip-toe to read it.

IT'S BIG. IT'S HUGE, said the letters at the top of the poster.

'It's Britt's *head*,' said Justin.

IT'S THE BEST PET PARADE IN THE WORLD!

'A Pet Parade?' said Big Mac.

'A Pet Parade?' said Fergus. 'How dull and boring!'

Warren shuddered. You could almost read his mind. Fleas. Rabies. Ringworm. Germs galore.

'Hey, wait on,' yelled Justin, 'it says we have to pay five dollars to enter. That's *robbery!* Five dollars to enter a dumb pet show?'

'But look at the prizes,' said Britt smugly, as she pinned up another list. Everyone looked. Then everybody started talking at once.

'Trip for two to Movie World and the Gold Coast? *Unreal!*'

'State-of-the-art computer? *Stoked!*'

'Dinner for two with Scott Michaelson? *Drool!*'

'Two hundred bucks worth of CDs? *Excellent!*'

Britt looked over all the heads at Rosie and shrugged. 'I knew I should've made the entry fee ten dollars,' she said, as her group handed out entry forms. Kids were *fighting* to get their hands on them!

'But I've got four pets,' said Horace Morris, 'so does that mean I've got to pay twenty dollars?'
'Right on, Mr H.'

'Well, they're all sure to win a prize,' said Horace happily. 'It'll be worth twenty dollars to go to Movie World and win the computer and the CDs. And maybe even one of the minor prizes.'

Because there were *more* . . . books, video games, tickets to movies, free meal vouchers, free roller-blading . . . the list was *big*.

'Where did she get all the money for the prizes?' said Big Mac. 'I know. Don't answer. Her father!'

'Yeah. His contacts. Probably got a brother who owns Movie World and a sister who owns Scott Michaelson,' said Boldy bitterly.

'You haven't grabbed a Pet form,' I said. I knew Boldy had a gorgeous King Charles spaniel that would've won first prize for the cutest dog hands down. Well, paws down.

'Wouldn't go in Britt's contest if you paid me!'

I sighed. I didn't want my friends missing out on good prizes just because Britt was being a Super-Boss. I grabbed a form.

'Whoa, Rosie. You haven't got a pet,' said Britt.

'She's buying one specially. A death adder. And it's going to be trained to bite *you*, Britt,' said Big Mac. Britt clenched her fist to punch Big Mac, then thought that wasn't such a good idea. A nudge from her could knock you into the middle of next week.

All this arguing was getting me depressed. I gave the form to Boldy.

'You have to enter. You have to win the contest, Boldy. You deserve the trip to Movie World for the cutest dog.'

'Well . . .'

'Go on, take it.'

'But . . .'

'It's for the good of the school and for the Eventide Home, remember.'

'Okay, then. But I haven't changed to Britt's side!'

The rest of the day was hectic. All the kids could talk about was the Pet Parade. It was being held on the following Friday at the school.

'Reporters and photographers will be here, of course,' said Britt, 'and maybe even TV cameras.'

'Der,' said Justin, but I could see that he was impressed.

Everyone was excited. Kids who didn't have pets were going to borrow them. There were big arguments, too. Did a bowl of goldfish count as one pet, or were they all individuals?

'How many goldfish?' asked Britt bossily.

'Seven. They're all very small.'

'That'll be thirty-five dollars, then.'

'That's dumb,' shouted Fergus, who'd been listening. 'If a dog has ten fleas coming along for the ride are you going to charge fifty dollars for them, too?'

57

'Oh,' moaned Warren, going green. 'Fleas? I feel *sick*. I'm not coming to the Pet Parade. I'll catch a fatal disease for sure. Fleas carry Bubonic Plague, don't you know that? We'll all get the plague and *die*. I've seen it on TV. You go blue and swell up like a balloon.'

He wandered off muttering to himself. He had to be the only weird kid in the whole school. Everyone else was keen to pay up their money because everyone was sure that his or her pet would win.

Miss Perret and Mr Cole started making plans. People had to bring their entry money and form by next Monday at the latest. They would mind the money.

'That's not fair,' said Britt angrily. 'It's *my* idea. It's *my* Pet Parade. *I* want to mind the money!'

Miss Perret looked at Mr Cole, then at Britt.

'You will *not* mind the money, Britt,' she said. 'There could be a thousand dollars or more. It will be put in Mr Walsnott's safe and banked in a special account.'

'So suffer, Britt!' whispered Boldy.

'What you can do instead is make some big lists of the entries in their sections, Britt,' said Mr Cole, 'so that everyone can *see* the entries. Once someone gives their money I'll give you the form and you and your group can be in charge of all those details.'

Britt seemed happier then. She would still be in charge. She would be the first person to see the forms. She would be the first person to know who was bringing particular pets. She would be writing the information on big lists. Fergus wriggled in his seat. He loved to know what was going on before everyone else. He was the biggest sticky-beak in the world! Britt saw him and smiled.

'Would you like to help me with the forms, Fergus? You could if . . . you were in my group!'

'Well, I'm not,' said Fergus.

'I'll let you come into my group. I'll let you be in charge of the forms,' said Britt.

There was a gasp. Everyone stared at Fergus. He went red. It was as though there was a big war going on inside him. He really wanted to see those forms before anyone else. He really wanted to know what was *going on* before anyone else.

'It's okay with me, Fergus,' I said.

He looked at me. Then he looked at Britt. He gave a big sigh.

'Go boil your bossy head, Britt. I wouldn't be in your group if it was the last one on the planet!'

Chapter Six

Junk for Sale

During the hustle and bustle of the Pet Parade planning I suddenly realised that we'd forgotten about fund-raising. Britt's group was roaring ahead collecting heaps of money. But it didn't mean that we had to give up. We could still make some money by working on another project. It didn't matter if we didn't win, but we had to keep going and make some *more* money for the Eventide Home for the Aged project!

'You gonna give up, Rosie?' said Britt. 'You may as well!'

'No way, Britt!' I said, even more determined.

The next day at school I sent round a note to my group, although the whole class read it. It said, 'We need to raise more money. Ideas? Meet at the shelter shed at morning recess.'

Britt grabbed the note off me and added in huge writing, GIVE UP OR DIE.

I wasn't going to give up. And I wasn't going to die. There had to be something . . .

Stacey thought of it just before morning recess, and told it to us when we all met. It wasn't in the shelter shed because she'd grabbed everyone just outside the door.

'A garage sale? Great idea,' I said.

'Yeah. Cool,' said Fergus. 'We get to see everyone else's junk.'

'I thought we could have it here at school,' said Stacey. 'We could bring all our junk, toys, games we've stopped playing with, old plates, stuff that our parents and brothers and sisters don't want . . .'

'It can't be a garage sale,' argued Worry Wart. 'There isn't a garage here. And there'd be germs all over *everything*.'

He shuddered in horror.

'We could use Mr Walsnott's carport,' said Kylie. 'There'd be bags of room if he shifted out all *his* junk.'

'We could leave it there and flog it off,' said Justin.

'Yeah. And his carport's real handy. Right next door,' said Horace.

'Okay. So who's going to ask him?'

'Not me.'

'Rosie, you're the group leader and the president of the project. *You* ask him,' said Boldy.

'Me?'

I could feel the blood draining from my face. I was scared stiff of Mr Walsnott. The way he yelled . . .

'HEY. YOU LOT DO YOU HAVE TO
STAND UNDER MY OFFICE WINDOW
MAKING ALL THAT NOISE DON'T YOU
KNOW I'VE GOT A SCHOOL TO RUN I
CAN'T THINK WITH YOU ALL YABBER-
ING AND IF YOU DON'T STOP RIGHT
NOW I'LL PEEL YOUR SOCKS OFF AND
STUFF 'EM DOWN YOUR THROATS.'

It was now or never. I was group leader and the
project president. I looked at his angry, red face
glaring from his top storey window.

'Mr Walsnott, could you kindly shift your car
one day soon so's we can use your carport for a
garage sale? Please? Oh, and some of your . . . er . . .
junk as well?' I was trembling with fright.

'A GARAGE SALE? WHAT DO YOU THINK THIS IS A CHARITABLE INSTITUTION FOR KIDS WHO WANT TO MAKE SPARE MONEY TO WASTE ON PINBALL MACHINES AND OTHER USELESS RUBBISH?'

'We want to make money for the Eventide Home for the Aged Fund-Raising Contest,' I said. 'The GO MANGO project.' I could feel myself beginning to tremble. His face turned purple. If he kept this up he'd have a massive heart attack and end up in the Eventide Home before we could raise the money to pay for his wheelchair.

'IN THAT CASE ALL RIGHT BUT IF YOU LEAVE ANY MESS AT ALL YOU'LL BE SCRUBBING IT CLEAN WITH TOOTH-BRUSHES DO YOU HEAR ME?'

'Yes, sir,' I said, as Worry Wart nearly fainted with the shock of his toothbrush being used to scrub a filthy garage floor.

'Now we have to make more posters,' grumbled Big Mac. 'This is getting *boring*.'

We made the posters at lunch-time and put them up next to the ones advertising the Pet Parade.

GARAJE SALE. BRING YOUR TRESHERS. BUY SOME MORE. CHEEP PRESENTS.

'That's not how you spell "garage" and "trea-sure" . . . or "cheap",' sneered Bossy Britt, as she read our notice. 'Anyway, when is this garage sale? And where?'

'On Thursday,' I said quickly, hoping she wouldn't decide to have one on Wednesday. She was so sneaky and I didn't trust her one bit.

'Well, no one'll come unless you put when and where,' she said sarcastically.

Gritting my teeth I wrote, THURSDAY, MR WALSNOTT'S CARPORT, 10 am.

'Mr Walsnott's carport? Who said you . . .'

'Aw, go put your head in a deep freeze so's your brain'll be frozen for posterity,' said Boldy.

She gave him a filthy look.

On Thursday we set up all our junk in Mr Walsnott's carport. We had some really great stuff: toys, books, games, ornaments, soaps and talcs that had been given as gifts and never used, jewellery, cushions, a toaster, a waffle iron, an elephant's foot umbrella stand, a big woven fan, and clothes of all sizes.

'I don't think we're allowed to sell clothes,' said Worry Wart. 'There's a health regulation that says . . .'

'Aw, forget it, Worry Wart. You're such a pain,' said Sticks. It was true. Sometimes Worry Wart could be like a big, wet sponge, landing *splat* on people's ideas.

The biggest surprise was from Mr Cole. He'd brought snakes pickled in jars and three stuffed lizards. They would sell for an absolute fortune.

'Can we have first go at buying the stuff?' asked Piggsy, who had his eyes on the big black snake with the red bands and on a video game – one of those hand-held ones. The batteries were still okay because he was playing with it.

'Okay,' I said. 'But nothing else, or we won't have any stuff left to sell.' Our garage sale was a *huge* success. We made one hundred and seventy-six dollars and ninety-five cents. Clear profit. And it had been the easiest thing to do.

Let me tell you, if you spend hours making toffees, fudge and marshmallows, or you spend hours running a baby photo contest, you are wasting your time. A garage sale is the best way to make money in a hurry.

There was a bit of stuff left over, so we held a Lucky Dip and charged fifty cents a go. Millie moaned because she drew out a mouldy lump of fur that Horace insisted was a lucky rabbit's foot without the claws. She screamed so loudly that Mr Walsnott came running.

'WHAT'S ALL THAT SCREAMING ABOUT IS SOMEONE BEING MURDERED AND STOP WAVING THAT DIRTY LUMP OF FUR AT ME MILLIE OR I'LL HAVE TO HAVE YOU FUMIGATED.'

Worry Wart agreed with him.

We now had a grand total of two hundred and seventy-seven dollars and sixty-one cents. It was good, but we would need a *miracle* to make more money than Britt's Pet Parade!

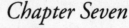

Chapter Seven
Big Mac's Plan

'I can't stand that bossy Britt,' said Big Mac, 'and now that she's making all this money with the Pet Parade, she's *worse!*' We were outside at recess time.

'I agree. She's bossier than ever,' said Justin.

'We need to do something else to keep up our spirits,' said Fergus. 'What do you reckon, Boldy?'

'Yeah. But what?'

'I've got an idea,' said Big Mac, looking excited. 'Britt's got over three hundred entries for the Pet Parade. There'll be mothers and fathers and grandparents and big and little brothers and sisters. There'll be a *crowd!* They'll get thirsty and

71

hungry. Plus there'll be thirsty, hungry pets, too. We could sell refreshments!'

'Great idea,' said Sticks enthusiastically. 'We could make *thousands!*'

'Well, maybe hundreds,' I said, 'but, remember, every little bit helps.'

'My dad'll donate the rolls for hot dogs and bread for sandwiches if I ask him,' said Big Mac. They had a bakery.

'Yeah. And mine'll give us the franks and the sausages, too, for a barbecue. Oh, and sliced ham to make sandwiches,' said Justin whose dad had a butcher's shop. 'And what about your mum and dad, Boldy? They could give some fruit and vegies from their shop.'

'Okay. And your dad takes soft drinks to places on his truck, Fergus. Maybe he could get some cans of Coke.'

'And my mum'll bake us cakes and slices,' I said. 'You know how she loves cooking.'

'I know. I know,' said Piggsy, rolling his eyes and clutching his stomach, 'but what could I bring?'

'What about me?' said Horace Morris.

'Maybe you two could set up water bowls for the dogs and sell pet snacks,' I said. 'Mr Sampson the pet shop man might donate some stuff.'

'Let's do it!'

'We'd better ask Miss Perret first. And we'll

Tee & coffee 20f

need help cooking the sausages and the franks. Oh, and do you think we should sell tea and coffee for the adults, too?' said Fergus.

Warren shuddered.

'I don't like eating food in the open air like that,' he said. 'The cooking smells bring *flies*. And flies are covered in *germs*.'

'You won't have to worry. You said you weren't coming!' snapped Big Mac.

'Oh, yes. That's right. So I did.' Worry Wart Warren cheered up then.

'I think we'd better make a list of the things we need to do,' I said, 'and we'll need paper cups and plates and a barbecue and trestles and . . .'

'What do you need trestles for, Rosie?'

It was Britt.

'It's a secret and not for *you* to find out!' said Big Mac in a bossy voice. She sounded nearly as bossy as Britt. We didn't need *two* bosses at Mango Primary!

'Yeah. Rack off, Bossy Boots,' said Justin, dodging around as Britt tried to pinch him.

'I heard you. Trestles. You're going to sell something,' said Britt, narrowing her eyes. 'Well, so long as it's not *before* my Pet Parade . . .'

'It's not,' blurted Sticks, falling for her trap. 'It's on the same day. We're doing the refreshments!'

'Ah. We'll see about *that!*'

Britt the Boss went rushing off towards the classroom.

Luckily for me, Miss Perret and Mr Cole thought it was a great idea. The Pet Parade wasn't just big any more. It wasn't huge. It was *mega-enormous!* Kids had even bought pets from Mr Sampson's pet shop so they'd have something to enter. There were sixty-seven dogs, eighty-four cats, thirty-nine birds, twenty-seven goldfish, eighteen rabbits, fifteen frogs, eleven turtles, a donkey, fourteen ponies, twelve guinea pigs, nine chooks and a rooster, three pigs, five lizards, three snakes, a possum, eighteen white mice, cockies, magpies . . . the list went on and on.

Mr Walsnott had decided to hire two big tents. Heaps of parents had volunteered to help with the organising and the judging. And everyone would need stuff to eat and drink!

The entry total was one thousand, six hundred and thirty-five dollars so far – clear profit!

'It's disgusting,' said Fergus.

'Yeah. Why didn't *we* think of it?' grumbled Big Mac.

'It wouldn't have done us any good if we had,' I pointed out. 'Britt didn't have to pay for the prizes, remember? We'd have to use the profits to buy stuff. We probably would've ended up with ten dollars!'

'Yeah. With our luck!' said Horace Morris gloomily.

'Well, at least it'll be clear profit for the food,' I said, as Britt sauntered past, nose in the air. She was totally full of herself: the whole thing had gone to her head. Even her group was starting to avoid her because she had become such a big pain.

It was Thursday, the day before the Pet Parade. The tents were already up and Mr Walsnott was losing it as usual, going off the planet, especially when some of the Grade One kids started pulling up the tent pegs to use for laser guns.

'WHAT DO YOU LOT THINK THIS IS SPACE INVADERS I'LL GIVE YOU ONE MINUTE TO GET THOSE TENT PEGS BACK OR IT *WILL* BE A WAR ZONE DO YOU HEAR ME?'

'He's gone really flaky,' said Sticks. 'I don't think he can stand the pressure.'

Then our supplies started arriving. Justin's dad brought heaps of sausages, franks and hamburgers, plus a stack of sliced cold meat. We had all these portable car fridges to store it in, lined up in the staff room. Fergus's dad brought cartons of

Coke plus several big fridges to keep it icy cold. Mum had been baking stacks of slices and cakes, and so had Horace's mum. Warren's parents had donated fully sterilised vacuum-packed paper cups and plates. And Big Mac's parents were bringing the fresh bread plus a heap of cakes and coffee scrolls in the morning. I felt scared when I saw the mountains of food. How would we cope? What if we couldn't sell it all? What if we couldn't eat it all? What if . . .?

'Keep calm, Rosie,' said Justin when I told him I was nervous.

'Yeah, stay cool,' added Stacey, bumping into the edge of the trestle table. 'What could possibly go wrong?'

Chapter Eight

Pets Galore

On Friday when we got to school it looked like the Melbourne Zoo. There were animals everywhere, and the judging didn't start till eleven o'clock! All the dogs were tied by leads to the bike racks with spaces between so they wouldn't fight. Then as more kept arriving they were tied to the fence. Just as well it wasn't hot weather. The cats were all in cages: Mr Walsnott had made that a Condition of Entry.

The dogs were all barking, the donkey was braying, the ponies were trying to gallop off home again, and someone's frog had escaped and was getting chased by the hungry rooster. Just as the

snapping beak got really close, the frog leapt up
onto Mr Walsnott's shoulder.

'WHAT ON EARTH IS THAT THING ON
ME UGH A FROG GET OFF ME YOU
SLIMY CREATURE FROM THE BLACK
LAGOON OR I'LL RIP OFF YOUR LEGS
AND HAVE THEM FRENCH-FRIED WITH
BUTTER AND GARLIC DO YOU HEAR
ME?'

'Oh, thank you for
catching Fiona,' said
this little Grade Two
kid, rushing up to
Mr Walsnott.
'Catching *who*?'
'Fiona. My frog.'

The frog gave a leap and landed on the little kid's head.

'It's her favourite spot, Mr Walsnott. She likes hair. She would've sat on *your* head if you'd had hair!'

'ERK I HATE FROGS I HATE KIDS WHO OWN FROGS NOW GET OVER THERE INTO YOUR LINE THE BELL'S ABOUT TO GO,' roared Mr Walsnott mopping at his coat with a large white handkerchief.

Then he charged up the steps as the bell rang and held up his hand.

'ALL PETS MUST BE TIED UP OR BE IN CAGES OR CONTAINERS AND NOT ROAMING AROUND ALL OVER THE PLACE OTHERWISE THEY WILL BE SENT HOME DO YOU UNDERSTAND ME?'

Hurriedly all these kids started stuffing their pets into cages, baskets or pockets. The noise was deafening.

'We'll have to shut the windows,' said Miss Perret once everyone was inside, 'or we won't be able to hear ourselves *think*.'

Fergus, Justin and Stacey were in charge of making sure all the dogs and ponies had water to drink. They gave all the dogs an icecream container of fresh water each. Some of the puppies were hopeless; they knocked over their containers straight away. The horses and donkeys had buckets.

'Look. What's that thing arriving?' said Fergus, as a car towing a trailer came in the school gate. Inside was . . .

'A goat! Who could possibly own a *goat*?' said Stacey.

'Baaaa,' bleated the goat, planting its four legs firmly and wagging its head from side to side. The lady led it across to the footy goal-posts and carefully put its chain round the base of the end post.

'There you go, Nanny,' she said.

'Who owns the goat?' asked Fergus, nosey as usual.

'I do, but my niece has borrowed her for the Pet Parade,' said the lady. 'I guess I'd better find her and tell her that Nanny's here. You wouldn't know which room Britt Blainey's in, would you?'

Fergus kept a straight face.

'Sure. Follow me.'

The lady walked off after him while Stacey and Justin looked at the goat. 'Baaaa,' she said, staring at them with her weird yellow eyes.

'She reminds me of someone.'

'Who? Britt?'

'You got it, kiddo,' said Justin.

'We'd better get back into school before the recess bell goes and Mr Walsnott starts yelling again,' said Stacey.

They'd just got back into the classroom when the bell rang and everyone else came stampeding out. The dogs started barking again even louder than before. The ducks quacked, the donkey threw back his head and brayed, and the noise just about lifted the roof off the school.

The teachers started putting everyone into groups for each different category. The dogs and cats were in separate sections in the biggest tent. The mice, guinea-pigs and frogs were in with the birds and lizards. Each had a special place. Britt had organised it extremely well!

Mr Walsnott was rushing round looking hot and flustered.

'THIS IS THE LAST PET PARADE WE'RE EVER HAVING AT THIS SCHOOL AGAIN EVEN IF IT HAS RAISED OVER A THOUSAND DOLLARS,' he yelled, bending down to retrieve a dog that had run away from its owner.

'Mr Walsnott. Look out!' I called.

But it was too late. Nanny the goat came charging through the tent opening. She'd managed to get free of the goal-post. If there was one thing she hated it was being tied up. And another thing she hated was people bending over in front of her with big, fat bottoms. Her head went down.

Wump!!! Blam!!! She rammed into Mr Walsnott's backside and sent him flying head first into the rabbits' cages. The doors flew open and four rabbits dashed out heading straight for the ducks and hens. The ducks quacked, panicking, and knocked over their cages. Nanny the goat went ripping through the tent wall. Animals were scattered everywhere. Kids were crying and trying to grab their pets.

More cages and baskets went flying. Mice scampered across the ground, guinea-pigs wuffled in fright and went scooting under the tent flaps. Lizards darted, frogs hopped, and Mr Walsnott bellowed with pain as he rubbed his sore behind. 'GET THAT GOAT. GET THAT GOAT.'

But Nanny the goat was enjoying her freedom. She'd gnawed through the base of the goal-post and escaped. She had no intentions of being captured and tied up again. She charged through the other tent, knocking over cats and dogs like pins in a bowling alley. Then she dodged the teachers who were trying to catch her and went roaring out the other side with pieces of torn tent dan-

gling from her horns. Three big dogs gave chase, yelping at the top of their lungs. This scared the ponies into a frenzy. They galloped madly round the oval, their broken reins dangling, pawing up great clods of beautiful newly sown grass. The

donkey stood petrified in the middle, braying his head off.

Rabbits and mice went zooming all over the place. Cats were chasing guinea-pigs and dogs were chasing cats.

Nanny the goat went tearing up the school
steps with a pack of yelping dogs behind her.
She ran into the art room. Bang. Crash.

Paint went flying all over the walls and floor. Nanny tore round the room with at least twelve dogs *and* Mr Cole trying to catch her. The dogs got covered in paint. Nanny wheeled round, through Mr Cole's outstretched arms, and bolted out the door and up the stairs. The dogs chased after her, paint dripping from their fur all over the floor, smearing it all over the walls as they followed in hot pursuit. Nanny skidded wildly from room to room, knocking over desks, shelves of books, pens and pencils . . . it was one *huge* mess.

The goat got to the Grade Six room – and so did the dogs. Mr Cole, puffing after the hectic chase, watched from the doorway in horror as Nanny took a flying leap through Warren the Worry Wart's window and went sailing through the air. The dogs stood panting, tongues hanging out, as their frantic owners rushed up the stairs and put their leads onto their collars.

'What happened to the goat?' said Horace Morris, looking at the mess in awe.

There was a big jagged hole where the window had been.

'Don't look,' said Mr Cole in a weak voice. 'It'll be . . . horrible.'

A goat leaping from the top storey onto the asphalt below wouldn't stand a chance. Miss Perret came panting up the stairs, white faced.

She groaned when she saw the mess.

'Oh, *no!*'

Then she saw the window.

'What . . .?'

'The goat!'

'The poor thing. Oh, how awful!'

But just then they heard, 'Maaa, maaa,' drifting up from below.

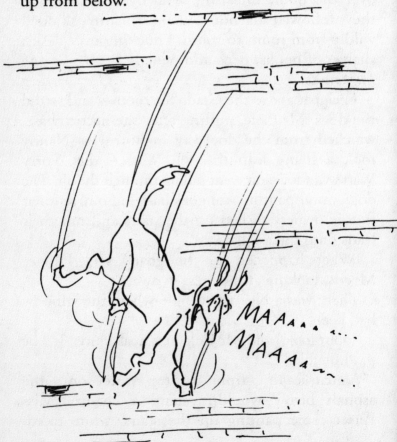

MAAAA.... ....
MAAAA~~...

Everyone rushed to the windows and looked down. Nanny the goat had landed with full force on the trestle table holding all the mountains of bread rolls and loaves. It had been like landing on a huge mattress! The trestle table had given way and collapsed, spilling all the sausages and franks and cakes onto the ground. Nanny was calmly chewing up the tablecloth. Three dogs were fighting over a string of sausages. Dogs, cats, chooks, and a big assortment of other pets were gobbling up all the food as fast as they could.

'Quick,' yelled Mr Cole, 'everyone. Downstairs.'

There was a mad scramble to get outside. Rosie, who'd rushed up after the others, collided with a man carrying a camera.

'Excuse me,' he said, looking bewildered, 'but is this Mango Street Primary School? I'm here to photograph a Pet Parade for the *Sun* newspaper.'

'Oh.'

Rosie looked wildly around. Then she spotted Mr Walsnott running across the yard trying to catch a bolting pony.

'There's the Principal, Mr Walsnott,' she yelled above the row. 'You'd better speak to him.'

Just then Mr Walsnott's foot landed in one of the water buckets. He rolled over and over, coming to land at the photographer's feet, the bucket still attached to his foot.

'Smile!' said the photographer, raising his camera, just as the donkey kicked over the fridge with all the Coke inside. Cans went rolling in all directions. One clonked Mr Walsnott on the head. There were animals and kids and parents and teachers and food and Coke cans all muddled together. What a *mess*.

Fergus was standing beside the table holding the urn, coffee, tea, milk and sugar. It was the only thing still standing.

'Er . . . would anyone like a cup of tea?' he said.

Chapter Nine

Britt the Boss

The Pet Parade was over.

All the animals and birds had been recaptured and taken home. A team of cleaners had been hired to clean up the mess, and carpenters, gardeners and a heap of other people were repairing the damage.

School was closed for the rest of the day. Yay!

The next day everyone arrived feeling apprehensive. The rooms were restored to order. The window was mended.

'Oh, *yuk!* said Worry Wart when he was told that a goat had jumped through his window. 'Did it stand on my seat? Did it drop any germs?'

He was busy for half an hour wiping everything with his special disinfectant and clean cloth which he carried in his school bag. He wiped the window ledge, his entire desk, and the floor all around him. He looked quite pale.

'You missed all the excitement, Warren,' said Stacey. Warren shuddered and closed his eyes.

Someone had brought the photos from the front page of the *Sun* newspaper. One showed Mr Walsnott getting clonked on the head with a Coke

can, and with his foot in the bucket. SCHOOL
PRINCIPAL INTO HEAVY METAL read the
caption. There was a photograph of the animals
eating the food. PET PARADE WITH A DIF-
FERENCE it said. There was another of Nanny
chewing up the tablecloth and the horses running
riot in the distance. 'NO KIDDING!' said the caption. And one of Miss Perret with her arms round Mr
Cole's neck screaming hysterically with a mouse
running up her arm. MOUSE PHOBIA AT
MANGO STREET it said.

'Boy! Wait till Miss Perret's boyfriend sees *that!*'
whispered Big Mac. 'Mr Cole will be *dead meat.*'

But worse was to come. Mr Walsnott called an
assembly. And he was *mad!* Real mad. He was

probably suffering from a bad headache. He had two band-aids stuck across his forehead with a large purple bruise showing underneath the edges.

'NEVER AGAIN WILL THERE EVER EVER BE A PET PARADE AT THIS SCHOOL IT WAS THE DUMBEST MOST STUPIDEST IDEA I'VE EVER COME ACROSS AND WHO WAS THE *DILL* WHO THOUGHT OF IT, WHO, WHO, WHO?' Tabitha scuffed her shoe against the asphalt. Obviously she hadn't told him anything, especially that *she'd* been in Britt's group.

'WHO? I KNOW IT WAS A GRADE SIX PROJECT I SAW THE POSTERS I KNEW ABOUT THE PRIZES BUT WHO WAS THE *IDIOT* WHO DREAMED UP THIS RIDICULOUS IDEA?'

Britt put up her hand.

'I SHOULD HAVE GUESSED YOU MISS BOSSY BREECHES ALWAYS BOSSING EVERYONE AROUND WELL YOUR BOSS-ING DAYS ARE OVER AND SO'S YOUR FUND-RAISING MONEY BECAUSE IT'S PAYING FOR ALL THE DAMAGE.'

Britt looked like she was going to cry.

'AND DO YOU KNOW HOW MUCH THE BILL COMES TO, MISS BOSSY? DO YOU? ONE THOUSAND FIVE HUNDRED DOL-LARS! THE INSURANCE COMPANY WON'T PAY AND THE EDUCATION DEPARTMENT

DEFINITELY WON'T PAY. WE ARE NOT INSURED FOR ANIMALS GOING BERSERK AND A GOAT JUMPING THROUGH A WINDOW. ISN'T IT LUCKY THAT I HAPPEN TO HAVE ONE THOUSAND SIX HUNDRED AND THIRTY-FIVE DOLLARS IN A BANK ACCOUNT! EH? EH? EH?'

He was so angry that everyone thought he would explode into a thousand pieces. Assembly ended. Everyone went back into class.

'No more Pet Parades,' said Boldy. 'Not fair. My spaniel would've won for sure.'

'He might have won the cutest dog but I would've won the most unusual pet,' said Piggsy.

'You haven't even *got* a pet.'

'Yes I have – the snake in the bottle!'

'Oh, *yuk!*

'Quiet. Get out your English books,' said Miss Perret.

Britt had her head down on the desk. She wasn't saying a word. I felt sorry for her. It must've been awful being yelled at by Mr Walsnott in front of the whole school. I gave her arm a gentle shake.

'Britt. Are you all right?'

She looked up. Her face was streaked with tears. 'Bet you feel good, Rosie. You won!' she said.

'Huh?'

'The Eventide Home for the Aged. Your group made more money. You won by one hundred and seventy dollars and sixty-five cents.'

I'd forgotten all about it. Oh, *no*. Now I'd have to take the money to the home and make a speech in front of lots of people. I didn't want to do it. And all those people had been relying on us getting lots of money. This was *awful*.

'I'm sorry, Britt.'

'Sure.'

She put her head down on the desk again. It must be terrible to be a leader and have everything go wrong, I thought. It must be terrible to be born bossy and then suddenly be squashed flat by someone like Mr Walsnott and made to look stupid. There had to be *something* . . .

Then I had an idea.

'The prizes!' I yelled. 'We can raffle off the prizes!'

'Rosie Tucker, be quiet!' snapped Miss Perret.

But I leapt to my feet and faced the class. 'We can raffle off all the prizes that were supposed to be for the Pet Parade. We can make lots of money for the Eventide Home for the Aged.'

'Hey. Great idea!' said Justin. 'It's *our* group's idea so we get the money to add to our total.'

I shook my head.

'No,' I said. 'I think this should be a *whole* class project, not a competition. I want to resign as group leader and president. There is only one person in this room who is a good enough organiser to do it well . . . and that person is Britt.'

are you sure, Rosie?

'Are you sure, Rosie?' said Mr Cole.

'Of course she's sure,' snapped Britt, raising her

OF course she's sure!

head and glaring at him. 'Now, what I think we should do . . . Piggsy, stop dreaming and listen . . . Rosie, give me your pencil . . . what we have to do is . . .'

I sat down in my seat and smiled to myself.

Britt *was* good at organising. We'd make *thousands*. Once a boss, always a boss! Well, I guess the

world needs leaders, so watch out, because
Britt the Boss is coming!

About the author

Margaret Clark is the author of *Pugwall* and *Pugwall's Summer* (also published by Penguin), which were made into two television series, now shown all over the world. Her other books are *The Big Chocolate Bar, Famous for Five Minutes, Plastic City, Fat Chance, Living with Leanne, Ghost on Toast* and *Hold My Hand – Or Else* (published by Random House) and *Tina Tuff, Ripper and Fang* and *Calvin the Clutterbuster* (published by Omnibus Books). She works full time as an Education Officer for the Geelong Community Health Services Alcohol and Drug Program, and writing humorous books for children and teenagers is her hobby. She is married with two grown-up children, has a heeler dog, two cats, and loves eating everything (except tripe), reading, writing, and snoozing on the beach.

Margaret's other books in the Mango Street series are *Butterfingers, Weird Warren* and *Wally the Whiz Kid*.

About the illustrator

Bettina Guthridge has illustrated many delightful books for children, both by Australian authors as well as stories by overseas writers such as Ogden Nash and Roald Dahl. Her first picture book was *Matilda and the Dragon*, followed by *Hurry Up, Oscar!* by Sally Morgan. Using pen and ink and watercolour, her fresh and lively illustrations are always popular with children and adults alike. Bettina lives in Melbourne with her family, and is a full-time artist.

THERE'S NUFFIN' LIKE A PUFFIN!

☆☆☆☆☆☆☆☆☆☆☆☆☆☆☆☆☆☆☆☆☆☆☆☆☆☆☆☆

ALSO BY MARGARET CLARK

Weird Warren   Margaret Clark/Illustrated by Bettina Guthridge

Weird Warren worries about *everything*. He drives all the kids in Year Six at Mango Street Primary School round the bend – in fact, he's a Major Problem for his friend Fergus. But then comes the Eskimo project, which has Warren stuck in more ways than one, and Fergus is determined to find him a cure!

Butterfingers   Margaret Clark/Illustrated by Bettina Guthridge

It isn't much fun being the clumsiest kid at Mango Street Primary School. Stacey 'Butterfingers' Martin sure has a problem, and it's a real hassle for everyone, especially Mandy. But after they go to the fun park for Mandy's birthday, something *very* weird happens. Or is the answer as simple as Mandy thinks it is?

Wally the Whiz Kid   Margaret Clark/
Illustrated by Bettina Guthridge

There's this kid in the class who's a real brain. Wally is super-intelligent, but he manages to get into some pretty complicated situations in this very funny Mango Street Story.

THERE'S NUFFIN' LIKE A PUFFIN!
✩✩✩✩✩✩✩✩✩✩✩✩✩✩✩✩✩✩✩✩✩✩✩✩✩✩✩✩

Elmer Runs Wild   Patrick Cook

Elmer returns to Mother Murphy's Fishburger Takeaway, only to find that standards have gone downhill, and Mother Murphy has started to sell nothing but squid. One night there is a fire, and Elmer is forced back to the wharves, where life is hungry and dangerous.

Wry Rhymes   Max Fatchen/Illustrated by Michael Atchinson

A collection of rhymes and verses which young children will love.

Bicycles Don't Fly   Barbara Giles/Illustrated by Randy Glusac

When Jack, champion billycarter, gets a bike for Christmas, adventures begin, with bandits and chases, races and rewards. With Bill to help him and Pug out to beat him, can he win the biggest billycart race in the country?

Flying Backwards   Barbara Giles/Illustrated by Lin Tobias

When the blue oil on Jack's old bike begins to work its magic, he and Pug are transported back one hundred years in time; they meet their ancestors, take part in a village fair and find enough gold to buy Jack a new BMX – if only they could get home . . .

THERE'S NUFFIN' LIKE A PUFFIN!
☆☆☆☆☆☆☆☆☆☆☆☆☆☆☆☆☆☆☆☆☆☆☆☆☆☆☆

I Hate Fridays!   Rachel Flynn/Illustrated by Craig Smith

A collection of stories about characters in the classroom, about all the funny, sad and traumatic things that can happen. Hilariously illustrated by the very popular Craig Smith.

A Children's Book Council of Australia Notable Book, 1991.

It's Not Fair!   Rachel Flynn/Illustrated by Craig Smith

More hilarious stories from the kids at Koala Hills Primary School. In this second book, following *I Hate Fridays*, you can discover more funny things about Kirsty, Sam and the others.

I Can't Wait!   Rachel Flynn/Illustrated by Craig Smith

It's the last year of primary school for the characters from Koala Hills. Following the huge success of *I Hate Fridays!* and *It's Not Fair!*, here are your favourite characters back again.

THERE'S NUFFIN' LIKE A PUFFIN!

☆☆☆☆☆☆☆☆☆☆☆☆☆☆☆☆☆☆☆☆☆☆☆☆☆☆

So Who Needs Lotto?   Libby Hathorn/Illustrated
by Simon Kneebone

When Denise Albermarle arrives at Mimosa Primary School, she
is such a show-off and a bully that everyone hates her. So when
she begins to strike up a friendship with shy Cosmo Ravezzi, no
one is more surprised than he is . . .

A Children's Book Council of Australia Notable Book, 1991.

The Lenski Kids and Dracula   Libby Hathorn/Illustrated
by Peter Viska

The Lenski kids are the wildest, naughtiest kids in the
neighbourhood – until Kim Kip arrives next door. She goes to
acting school and is saving for a Harley Davidson motor bike,
and is keen to do some babysitting . . .

Old Tom   Leigh Hobbs

Old Tom is a lovable, battle-scarred, naughty but wickedly
appealing old tom cat. Here are his adventures, told with a witty
text and hilarious illustrations!

THERE'S NUFFIN' LIKE A PUFFIN!
☆☆☆☆☆☆☆☆☆☆☆☆☆☆☆☆☆☆☆☆☆☆☆☆☆☆☆

The Cabbage Patch Fib   Paul Jennings/Illustrated by Craig Smith

When an embarrassed Dad tells Chris that babies grow out of cabbages, Chris searches the vegetable garden – where he finds a baby. Being an instant father is okay for a while, but Chris soon tires of parental responsibility, until his problem is solved in an hilarious way.

Winner of the 1989 Young Australians' Best Book Award (YABBA), Victoria.
Winner of the Canberra's Own Outstanding List Award (COOL), ACT.

The Paw Thing   Paul Jennings/Illustrated by Keith McEwan

The stomach of a cat is no place for a miniature radio, especially when it is switched on. A takeaway chicken shop is not the ideal home for a million mice. And 'Dead Rooster' is not an ideal name for a takeaway chicken shop. But in this crazy story you will find them all.

Winner of the 1990 Young Australians' Best Book Award (YABBA), Victoria.
Winner of the 1991 West Australian Young Readers' Book Award (WAYRA).

The Gizmo   Paul Jennings/Illustrated by Keith McEwan

Some gizmos are pretty weird, but this one is the weirdest ever! And it won't go away. A wacky new story by the amazing Paul Jennings.

THERE'S NUFFIN' LIKE A PUFFIN!
☆☆☆☆☆☆☆☆☆☆☆☆☆☆☆☆☆☆☆☆☆☆☆☆☆☆☆☆☆☆☆

The Twenty-Seventh Annual African Hippopotamus Race
Morris Lurie/Illustrated by Elizabeth Honey

Eight-year-old Edward trains very hard for this greatest of swimming marathons with no idea of the cunning and jealousy he'll meet from the other competitors. This best-selling story takes you behind the scenes and shows you just what it takes to become a champion.

Winner of the Young Australians' Best Book Award (YABBA) 1986.

Cowboy Joe and the Bucking Barrel   Paty Marshall-Stace/Illustrated
                                              by Kevin Burgemeestre

Uncle Joe is a cowboy from Wyoming who rides bucking bulls and says, real slow and polite, 'Why, howdy partner.' And his nephews can't guess what fun's in Uncle Joe's bucking barrel!

The Magic Caravan   Paty Marshall-Stace

In lyrical poetic prose and with tender, evocative illustrations, Paty Marshall-Stace tells the story of a neglected bondwood caravan that shapes the lives of a young family.

THERE'S NUFFIN' LIKE A PUFFIN!
☆☆☆☆☆☆☆☆☆☆☆☆☆☆☆☆☆☆☆☆☆☆☆☆☆

The Black Duck   Eleanor Nilsson/Illustrated by Rae Dale

When Tom and his family move from their farm at Kangarilla, Tom has to leave his much loved pet behind – a little wild black duck called Squeak Toy. But, mistakenly, he thinks that Squeak Toy will be returned to him on his birthday, and when she isn't, he sets out to find her . . .

Shortlisted for the 1991 CBC Book of the Year Award for Younger Readers.

The Giant's Tooth   Gillian Rubinstein/Illustrated by Craig Smith

One day, during their summer holidays, Tania and Troy find a giant tooth on the beach. Beside it, scrawled in the sand, is a mysterious message . . .

Shortlisted in the 1994 CBC Book of the Year Awards.

Flashback: the Amazing Adventures of a Film Horse
Gillian Rubinstein

Antony and his pony Flash accidentally stumble into the world of the movies, a world full of villains and heroes and heart-stopping adventure.

A Children's Book Council of Australia Notable Book, 1991.